D1089052

THE
MIRACLE
OF THE
MOUNTAIN

By Rudyard Kipling
Adapted by Aroline Beecher Leach

Illustrated by Willi Baum

Addison-Wesley

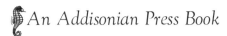An Addisonian Press Book

ADDISON-WESLEY PUBLISHING COMPANY, INC.

Reading, Massachusetts

The Miracle of the Mountain has been adapted from a longer
story, *The Miracle of Purun Bhagat,* by Rudyard Kipling.

Text copyright © 1969 by Aroline Beecher Leach
All rights reserved.
Illustration copyright © 1969 by Willi Baum
All rights reserved. Except for use in reviews,
no illustrations from this book
may be reproduced, utilized or transmitted
in any form or by any means,
electronic or mechanical, including
photocopying, recording, or by any information
storage and retrieval system,
without permission in writing
from the Publisher.
Library of Congress catalog card number 69–15801
Printed in the United States of America
First Printing

61719

BELMONT COLLEGE LIBRARY

Juv
PZ
7
L457
Mg

THE
MIRACLE
OF THE
MOUNTAIN

Rudyard Kipling

There was once
a wealthy man in India
whose name was Purun Dass.
After a full
and busy life
serving his country,
he gave up great riches
and honor,
took up the begging bowl
and saffron robe,
and walked out of his city
barefoot and alone
to be a holy man.

He followed his dream of peace
and quiet along the long,
white, dusty Indian road,
with the slow bullock carts
and the smell of wood-smoke
curling up under the fig trees
in the evening.

Sometimes he spread his blanket on the outskirts of a little Hindu village, where the children brought him food their parents had prepared;

sometimes he slept near the camels on the bare grazing grounds.

But his feet drew him slowly northward
and eastward, till one day he saw
the far line of the great Himalayas.

Then
Purun Dass
smiled,
for he
remembered
that
his
mother
was a
Hill-woman,
always
homesick
for
the snows.

"Yonder," said Purun Dass, "I shall sit down
and get knowledge"; and the cool wind of the Himalayas
whistled about his ears as he trod the road
up the mountains. For two days he climbed,
and in the evening crossed a high pass and came out
on a line of snow peaks that banded all the horizon.
The pass was crowned with dark forest trees,
and under the trees stood a deserted shrine to Kali.

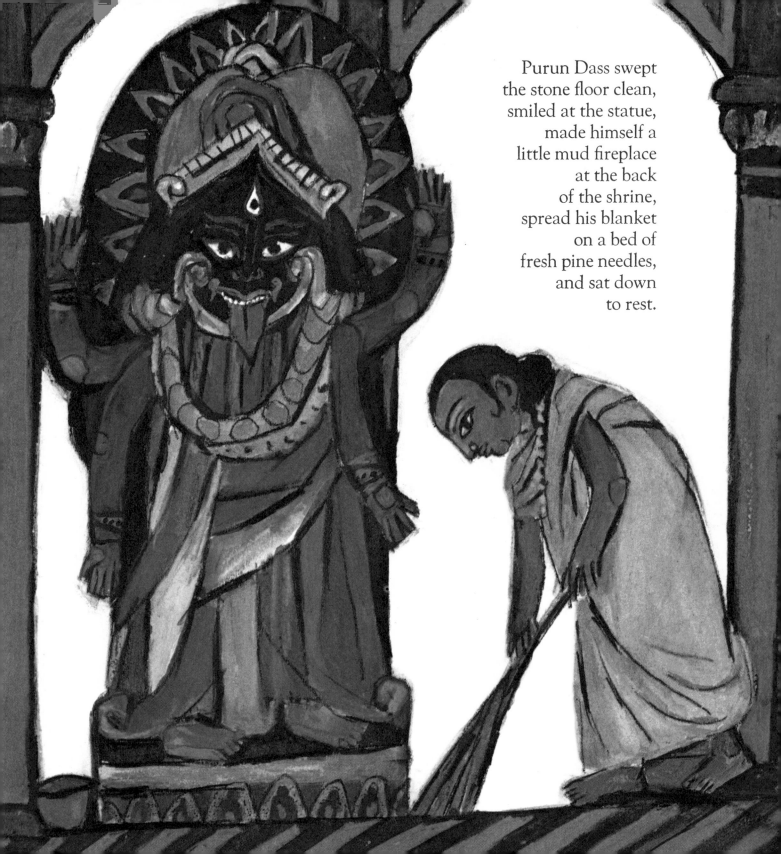

Purun Dass swept
the stone floor clean,
smiled at the statue,
made himself a
little mud fireplace
at the back
of the shrine,
spread his blanket
on a bed of
fresh pine needles,
and sat down
to rest.

Below him the hillside sloped down steeply,
and a little village of stone-walled houses clung to the slope,
with tiny terraced fields like aprons of patchwork
on the knees of the mountain,
and cows looking no bigger than beetles.

"Here shall I find peace," said Purun Dass.

As soon as the villagers saw
the smoke in the deserted shrine,
the village priest climbed up
the terraced hillside
to welcome the stranger.
Then he returned
to the village, saying,
"We have at last a holy man.
Never have I seen such a man!"
Then all the housewives said,
"Think you
he will stay with us?"
and each did her best to cook
the most savory meal for him,
with corn, rice, honey,
apricots, and wild ginger.
Every day Purun Dass placed
his bowl outside the shrine,
and daily he was fed.

That was the end
of Purun Dass's wanderings.
He had found his place—
the silence and the space,
the time to think.
He never went to the village,
laid out like a map at his feet,
but could watch
the sowing and the harvest
and all the changing colors
of the seasons.

Very soon
the wild things,
who knew the shrine well,
came to look
at the intruder.

First came the langurs,
the big gray-whiskered
monkeys of the Himalayas,
because they are
alive with curiosity;
and when they had
upset the begging bowl,
and rolled it
around the floor,
and made faces
at the statue,
they decided that
the human being
who sat so still
was harmless.
At evening they would
leap down from the pines
and beg with their hands
for things to eat.
They liked the warmth
of the fire too,
and sometimes
in the morning Purun Dass
would find a furry monkey
sharing his blanket.

After the monkeys came the barasingh, the big deer,
who wished to rub off the velvet of his horns
against the cold stones of Kali's statue,
and stamped his feet when he saw the man at the shrine.
But Purun Dass never moved, and little by little
the royal stag edged up and nuzzled his shoulder.

Purun Dass slid one cool hand along the hot antlers,
and the touch soothed the fretted beast, who bowed his head,
and Purun Dass very softly rubbed and ravelled off the velvet.
Afterward, the barasingh brought his doe and fawn—
gentle things that mumbled on the holy man's blanket—
or would come alone at night to take his share of fresh walnuts.

Others came,
even Sona,
the Himalayan
black bear,

who came for a share
of the caresses and a dole
of bread or wild berries,
and Purun Dass called them
all his brothers.

So the years passed,
the fields changed
their colors,
the priest
grew older,
and many of
the children who
used to come
with the food
for the begging bowl
sent their own
children now;
and when you asked
the villagers
how long
their holy man
had lived in
Kali's shrine
at the head
of the pass,
they answered

"Always."

Then came such summer rains as had not been known in the Hills for many seasons. Through three good months the valley was wrapped in cloud and soaking mist—steady, unrelenting downfall, thunder-shower

after thunder-shower. Kali's shrine stood above the clouds, for the most part, and there was a whole month in which Purun Dass never caught a glimpse of his village.

All that time he heard
nothing but the sound
of a million little waters,
overhead from the trees
and underfoot along the ground,
soaking through the
pine needles and spouting
in newly-torn muddy channels
down the slopes.
Then the rains gathered
for their last downpour
and the water fell
in sheets and
leaped back in mud.
Purun Dass heaped his
fire high that night,
for he was sure his
brothers would need warmth;
but never a beast
came to the shrine,
though he called and called
till he dropped asleep.

It was in the black heart of the night,
the rain drumming like a thousand drums,
that he was roused by a plucking at his blanket,
and felt the little hand of a monkey.
"It is better here than in the trees,"
he said sleepily, loosening a fold of blanket,
"take it and be warm."
The monkey caught his hand and pulled hard.
"What is it? What is thy trouble, Brother?"
said Purun Dass.
"Look, even the barasingh
comes for shelter!"

The deer's antlers clashed
against Kali's statue
as he strode into the shrine.
He lowered them at Purun Dass
and stamped uneasily.

"Hai! Hai!
What is this?"
said Purun Dass.
But the deer pushed
him toward the door,
and as he did so
Purun Dass heard
the sound of something
opening with a sigh,
and saw two slabs
of the floor draw away
from each other,
while the sticky earth
below smacked its lips.
"Now I see,"
said Purun Dass.
"No blame to my brothers
that they did not sit
by the fire tonight.
The mountain is falling.
And yet—
why should I go?"

Then his eye fell on the begging-bowl
and his face changed.
"They have given me good food daily since I came,
and if I am not swift,
tomorrow there will not be one soul in the valley.
Indeed, I must go and warn them below.
Lend me thy neck, brother—
for I have but two feet."

Purun Dass lighted a pine torch
at the fire with his right hand,
clutched the neck of the great
deer with his left hand,
and stepped out into
the desperate night.
More of his brothers joined them,
the monkeys, and Sona the bear,
and they poured down
the steep muddy path
to the crooked village street.

Here Purun Dass
beat on the windows
of the first house,
as his torch blazed up.
"Up and out!"
he cried,
and he did not
know his own voice,
for it was years
since he had spoken
aloud to a man.
"The hill falls!
The hill is falling!
Up and out,
oh, you within!"

"It is our holy man," said the wife. "He stands among his beasts.
Gather the little ones and give the call."

The call spread from house to house. The people hurried into the street.
In the glare of the torches they saw
their holy man, the barasingh, the monkeys, and Sona, the bear.

"Across the valley
and up the next hill!"
shouted Purun Dass.
"Leave none behind!"

Then the people ran
as only Hill folk can run,
for they knew that
in a landslip you must
climb for the highest ground
across the valley.
They fled, splashing through
the little river
at the bottom,
and panted up the terraced
fields on the far side,
while the holy man
and his brothers followed.

At last the great deer
stopped in the shadow
of a deep pine wood,
five hundred feet
up the hillside, where
his instinct told him
he would be safe.

Then there was a sigh
in the air that grew
to a mutter, and a mutter
that grew to a roar,
and a roar that passed
all sense of hearing,
and the hillside on which
the villagers stood was hit
in the darkness
and rocked to the blow.
The very roots of the pines
quivered to the sound;
then it died away
to the sound of the rain
on soft earth.

When the day came the villagers looked across
the valley and saw that what had been forest
and terraced field and grazing ground was one raw,
red fan-shaped smear. Of the village, the shrine,
and the forest, there was no trace.
For one mile in width and two thousand feet
in depth the mountain side had come away bodily,
planed clean from head to heel.

Then the priest said to the villagers,
"Behold a miracle! Our holy man and his beasts
have saved our lives! Therefore now we will
build a temple in his honor in this place."

So before the year was ended
they built a temple there,
in a peaceful spot halfway up the mountain;
and always, every day,
they brought lights and flowers
and food to their holy man,
and the animals, his brothers.

THE
END